WX Rn

D0178120

700033936874

Odd Job Frog

To Dr Matt Lamb

Matador
9 Priory Business Park
Kibworth Beauchamp
Leicestershire LE8 0RX, UK
Tel: (+44) 116 279 2299
Fax: (+44) 116 279 2277
Email: books@troubador.co.uk
Web: www.troubador.co.uk/matador

ISBN 978-1784622-725

British Library Cataloguing in Publication Data.
A catalogue record for this book is available from the British Library.

Printed and bound in Malta by Gutenberg Press Ltd
Typeset in 17pt Arial by Troubador Publishing Ltd, Leicester, UK

Matador is an imprint of Troubador Publishing Ltd

Odd Job Frog

Colleen and Zed Jacey

"I'm bored," said Frog. "Bored, bored, **BORED**."

"Well you'd better get used it," his friend, Mouse, replied lazily. "Nothing exciting is going to happen in the middle of this field."

"You're right!" Frog jumped up. "But the city is full of exciting things. I'll go there."

"Look at that," Frog cried as he leapt around London.
"And this, and…Wow…

There are so many things to do.
Where shall I start?"

"But… oh dear."
Frog sat still.
"They all cost money
and I haven't got any.
I'll have to get a job."

The man in the Job Centre frowned at Frog. "We don't normally find jobs for frogs." He looked down his list. "You could try the Zoo."

The Head Zoo Keeper shook his head. "I'm sorry. You're simply too small to muck out the elephants or feed the lions," he said. Then he smiled. "But there might be something you could do."

Frog liked his job
cleaning the
animal's teeth
until…

Frog leapt into the air as the crocodile's jaw clamped shut.

SNAP!

"I know I wanted life to be more exciting," Frog said shakily. "But that doesn't include being eaten alive. There must be a safer job I can do."

"This job is better," Frog said.
He rubbed the jewel until it shone.
"It's much less dangerous."

But he spoke too soon.

Frog tried lots of other jobs…

…but something always went wrong.

"Oh dear," said Frog
as he trudged through
the city streets.
"The man in the Job
Centre was right.
There simply aren't
jobs for frogs in London."

Frog darted out of the way of a speeding taxi.
"And I miss my quiet field back home."

Frog walked on.
Then he stopped, and blinked.
What was a big green field
doing in the middle of the city?

"It *is* nice here." Frog sighed and lay down on a lily pad. "But I can't stay long. I still need a job if I'm going to visit the exciting sights of London."

"Ouch!" Something hard hit Frog on the head
and disappeared into the lake
with a loud…

Frog dived in after it.

He stared at hundreds of round white balls.

"Where did they all come from?"

He picked one up and climbed back onto his lily pad.

"You've found my golf ball!" a delighted voice shouted.
"Will you swap it for this pound?"

Frog smiled at the shiny coin.
"I can earn lots of money diving
for golf balls here," he said.
"It's an odd job but perfect for a frog."

The End